# MOM AN SECF

CW00419039

(Taboo Sex Stories Book 4)

**Luca Lincoln**

# Table of Contents

# Content Warning

This book contains explicit sexual content and should only be read by those who are of legal age to do so. Some topics contain a lot of bad languages. There isn't a single one of the characters under the age of eighteen!

# MOM AND SON SECRET

However, the re-appearance of a long-forgotten family member tore our love nest apart. The phone rang out of the blue on a weekend afternoon. This is Henry, isn't it? " A nice salesman's voice inquired.

"Uh... yeah." I had no idea who it was.

"Hello, this is Dennis, your father." The odds are that you have forgotten about me, but you can bet the botHenry dollar that I have. How are things going? "Say, I think I should call my mother."

I went to Cathy and said, "There's a man on the phone, and he claims to be my father," and she agreed.

A burst of color faded from her face as she froze in place. When she realized what had happened, she closed her eyes. "What could he possibly...?" she said. When her hand reached her mouth, her teeth pressed carelessly on the thumb's knuckle in distraction. She got up after shaking her head and clearing her throat. She said, "I'll talk to him." with firmness.

What were they talking about that she didn't want me to hear when she shut the door to the living room?

When she came out, I was sulking in the kitchen. Her chin drooped because her face had been pinched. She briefly focused on me before moving on. Your father has spent a long time in prison. He's just walked out the door. "

I'm not sure what he wants. I raised an eyebrow when I inquired.

As far as I know, he'd like to start a family.

Fear tightened its grip on my gut. His target was obvious: her! Just what I was looking for. What if she was more attracted to him than I was? She was fond of him and enjoyed spending time with him. That's how I ended up here, after all. I asked, "Why did he go to prison?" because I wanted to cast him in a negative light.

"I'm not sure," Cathy replied. In the evening, "Perhaps he'll tell us."

"Tonight?"

Dinner will be served to him. "He's arriving."

Tension crept up my neck and chest as the threat loomed largely. As if he hadn't been invited before. My voice had begun to break. "Why didn't you ask me first?"

She looked at me with a perplexed expression. If you'd like to meet him, I'd be happy to. He is your father! "

No, I don't want to. Despite my best efforts, it came across as an allegation.

"Well... yeah. Inquiring minds want to know what's going on with him now. " Cathy had a great deal of respect for me. Her thick chestnut hair flowed over her shoulder, and she grabbed her chin with her small fist as she leaned her head backward. "Henry, what's the matter with you?"

My skin became flushed. "No! The problem is that She kissed my cheek while holding both of my hands in hers. "Don't be concerned. I stopped caring about Dennis years ago. When she looked at me, her gaze wrapped around me, and my dread subsided. "His gift was you." To me, he's only significant because of that. " She put her hands around my wrists and jerked my arms in a jerky motion as she tried to get me to relax. We must, however, see him. In particular, you. Your father should be familiar with you. "

He is my dad. The way he was, what he was doing now, his thoughts on me, and the fact that he never made an effort to get in touch with us made me wonder about him. Afterward, I'd look in the mirror and see myself in the photos of him. Upon closer inspection, I could not discern any likeness, but it occurred to me that I might grow up to look somewhat like him. He appeared to be alright.

His poems were in Cathy's possession. I'd read them a long time ago and remembered liking them, despite my initial reaction of finding them strange. One of them, "Cascade Mountain Fights Back," was even etched into my brain.

Moonworts with sphagnum moss, fiddleneck maidenhairs

While pikas chirp in retaliation,

In the night's double-bitted sprawl The Widows of Ptarmigan are preparing to encircle you. What do you do? You're desired.

However, since the Man of the Hour was only in town for one hour,

The battle is done and dusted.

You're already dead, so they can't do anything to you.

You can't be imprisoned since you hold the keys.

You can, however, become irrationally obsessed with them.

with an endless supply of agoraphobia

in addition to heartbreaking vintage Mescalero songs.

I had no idea what it meant. That could have been one of the reasons I found it appealing. He had written it and he was composing more bizarre poetry somewhere else, which made me happy. He was this enigmatic figure lurking in the shadows. While I thought he was a jerk for leaving without saying goodbye, his disappearance piqued my interest.

That was, of course, before my mother and I got romantically involved. It was now clear to me that Dennis Funk was only going to bring a difficulty to my life.

It's been a long time since we've seen each other. Even so, I'm aware that it was my fault. Please accept my apologies for the inconvenience. Please accept my sincere gratitude for inviting me to your home. " When he arrived at the apartment that night, he stated The hoarseness in his voice sandpapered the corners of his words. After shaking his hand, Cathy kept her arm outstretched to prevent an embrace.

He was around six feet tall, which pleased me. That means I'd likely grow a few inches, as I'm now only 5-foot-8. His teeth were discolored and yellow when he smiled. In addition to his lengthy sideburns, droopy mustache, and whiskers under his lower lip, he possessed short, straight black hair. The lack of sunlight in prison may have contributed to his pale appearance. It didn't matter how young he was; he had a wrinkled and turned-down face. He had a twisted nose due to a fractured nose blade. His eyes were a clear, harsh, brittle blue, and they kept flitting about, unable to look into yours for more than a second. "This must be little Henry," he remarked. I was immediately enraged by his use of the word "small," but I still shook his hand, wanting to give him a hard hold. His hand felt chilly. You asked me, "How are things going, son?"

"OK."

When I last saw you, you were a baby. Your current age is "

"Eighteen."

As far as I can tell, it is a wonderful age to be in. When I was eighteen, I recalled... Wistful sighs could be heard on his long, thin face as his voice faded. "You're too young to know better, aren't you?"

"I think so," I answered, recalling my conversation with my mother last night.

Let me tell you something: "Hell... I spent half that time in slam." In an instant, his smile turned into a frown. He wore a denim shirt, skinny pants, a canvas belt, and black, clunky shoes to cover his slender frame. That's what you get when you're released from prison.

What's the purpose of this? If it wasn't murder, I was looking for something that would truly pique her interest.

When I asked him about it, he looked at me like I was crazy and said, "I'll tell you later." His words suggested that he intended to remain.

The pale lipstick and black leotard Cathy was sporting were probably a throwback to her Beatle days. Her red hair, which brushed her breasts, looked stunning against the black of her outfit. Since the costume was so tight, it was easy to see her trying to turn Dennis on. With her all black and him all blue, I had to admit that they looked good together.

On the spur of the moment, I went into my room and changed into a black T-shirt. Because of my jeans, I looked like a cross between a black and a blue person.

Dennis was chatting with Cathy when I returned. "You get a little scared when you've spent so much time in a cell." To get out of this mess, I need to know every option available. "

I told him in my head that the door was right there, and then I apologized for being so cruel.

As long as I don't get too claustrophobic, would you mind if I take a look around? He apologized with a shrug as he tugged on the tuft of whiskers behind his lip.

When he asked whether she would show him around, she nodded cautiously, as if understanding. Cathy was well-acquainted with the jitters that many newly released convicts experience.

I wanted to tell her that he's probably just checking things out.

An ancient brownstone in downtown Denver's Uptown neighborhood offered us a room on the top floor with a view of the gold-domed Colorado State Capitol. As compared to a prison cell with its lofty ceilings, huge windows, and polished oak floors covered in vibrant carpets, this was a room that seemed like home. As Dennis strolled through it, his thumbs were tucked into the pockets of his jeans, and he grinned gleefully at the sight of everything that it had to offer. A tic on the right side of his face would cause him to blink his right eye every so often. After last night's raucous incestuous screams, he gave my mother's queen-sized bed a look that could only be characterized as focused. He lifted his brows and smacked his yellow teeth together as he looked around the bedroom. "Cathy, you did a fantastic job." What a wonderful place to grow up! It has been a long time since we lived in the tiny apartment in Five Points.

When she responded, "Well... it wasn't easy being a single mother," he winced and turned away to avoid looking at her.

Reconciling himself, he turned and looked back at her with a stoic expression. "The worst mistake I ever made was to abandon you, to abandon you in such a way that you had no recourse." Henry, you're included as well. In retrospect, I wish I'd stayed and assisted you both. "

It was difficult to see how he could have been of assistance. "What happened?" I savagely ripped at him.

Through the walls, he saw me. That was so long ago...I'm not sure.

"Well," Cathy remarked, "I'm guessing you're starving." Eat, please. "

"Yeah!" His mustache was brushed back.

In the beginning, we used forks to eat an antipasto tray with artichoke hearts and olives, as well as cheese, salami, cherry Henryatoes, and jalapenos. Once the pasta and salad were finished, we split our attention between the two dishes, which were served with garlicky sausage and a vinaigrette-based dressing.

"Hallelujah! There you go! You've mastered the art of cooking. " She was treated like a dessert by Dennis, whose mouth was stained red from Henryato sauce. He replenished his wine glass from the straw-wrapped Chianti bottle and savored every mouthful. A far cry from the Red Mountain rotgut we used to consume,

"Mmm... a lot better."

The wine's sour-bitter flavor didn't appeal to me at all. When fresh grape juice was so much better, why consume rotten juice?

Many thanks! It wasn't long until Dennis was slumped back in his chair with his eyes glazed over. "I'd like to express my gratitude to those who

Ma'am, I'd want to speak with you. Best lunch I've had in a long time! I don't know when I'll be able to get back to you. Permitting me to puff on one of your cigarettes would be greatly appreciated. "

Cathy shook her head and sighed. "It's fine." She climbed out of her chair and rummaged through a drawer till she came across an ashtray. It bothered me, but it made no difference. I opened the window. Rolling papers and a pouch were found in Dennis's pocket, and he began to roll a joint. I grew more alert, but it was Bull Durham.

He said, "So... you've got a boyfriend?"

She fixed her gaze on mine, a smirk creeping across her lips. "No. In any case, I'm not actively searching for one.

"Oh." He crossed his long legs and tugged at his whiskers once more. When I saw this shady person, I wanted to know more about him.

Because he was my father, I was eager to learn from him. He had let wine and food loosen him up, and he was grateful that someone cared enough to inquire. His ancestors immigrated to St. Paul, Minnesota, from Boston, Massachusetts, via Ireland. Jack Frye was his full name. When he decided to become a poet, he studied English for three years at Carlton College. When he worked in Washington State, he was disgusted by the practice of clear-cutting forests. As a kind of protest, he penned "Cascade Mountain Fights Back." He was dealing a lot of grass and peyote by this point, which he had smuggled into the US from Mexico. For the first time, he met his mother during a marketing trip to Denver. His importing business grew to include hashish from North Africa after he was startled by the home situation and divorced, the worst mistake of his life. After that, he committed the second-worst error. It wasn't long until his work for the syndicate paid off. The fuzz still needed a bust now and then to keep the chiefs off their backs despite bribing the narcs. As a result of this, Dennis was set up for a fall, and then committed to Attica for five years without parole. His nine-year sentence is more than that of some killers since he was caught in a shakedown after he had some heroin in prison.

I was sad for him since he'd had a bad experience, but he

was still unsettling because he kept looking around as if someone was following him.

No, I don't think so. I inquired about it.

When I questioned him, he seemed disappointed and I could tell he wished he hadn't. "Yes, I'm constantly working on new poetry. This is my new profession: writing in the clouds. "

"Tell me a story."

They take off as I write them. It's an absolute must that you attend. You have to be there to appreciate it. And it's only getting better... My life is my poem...." Then he looked at Cathy, who was sitting glumly. "What I'd like to know is..." I know you've got a wonderful, compact scenario here, but I blew my opportunity to participate. In the end, it's too late for me to get in on the action.

Understand? However, if I could simply stay here for the night. Cathy squinted her eyes at him and began to speak, but he went on speaking quickly. "I have no other place to stay at the moment." In the morning, I'll be gone. Promise. "

She took a deep breath, looked dissatisfied, and added, "Just for tonight, I guess." Unfortunately, we aren't ready for guests at this time.

Dennis breathed a sigh of contentment. "Thanks, The bus terminal would have kept me up all night if it weren't for your kindness. "

At the time, I was enraged. I had no idea he was going to sleep here. He's supposed to be leaving any minute now. He could return in seventeen years to check on our progress. This was the day we spent with family and friends on Saturday. I was looking forward to another night of fun with Mom today after we had such a fantastic time yesterday night. Who was he to interrupt our relaxing weekend?

Nonetheless, she set up a couch in the living room for him, and we all went to sleep together afterward. To keep an eye out for him sneaking into her room, I left my door open. I vowed to remain up all night in hopes of saving her from this vile rapist. However, at some point, I dozed off.

So when I awoke to find them both already awake, I began to wonder what had occurred. The images of my mother and Dennis were torturing me, and I couldn't help it.

I was enraged when she cooked waffles. Just how could she serve him our special breakfast? She even included amoretto in them; the only vanilla extract I ever received was from her. Why was she treating him so well if she didn't want him to stay?

Afterward, we sat at the same table where she had just leaned over so that I could take her from the back. Even though she was closer to me than Dennis, she was now in the middle of Dennis and myself, and it was something I loathed. Rather than face him, she should have sat on the other side of the room.

Even though I was sorry for my father, I could not appreciate him. I hoped to see him in Mexico or Tangier, but he said he was staying in Denver since it was where he had nice memories, the happiest time of his life, and a place to start again.

In Cathy's network of companies that recruit ex-convicts, she promised to try to get him a job.

He was extremely impressed by her work as a public defender. "The cops and DAs will have a field day with you." If you had been my attorney, you would have gotten me out of this situation. I would never have gone to the bar. "

She gave a shaky sigh. "Let's not even try it. Don't get the notion that you'll be returning to dealing. I can feel the sun beating down on me... and it's getting harder and harder. And Canon City isn't much better than Attica in this respect."

"Not to worry, I've got it under control." He rose up. "Stayin' clean... like a desert bone." As promised, I'll be on my way. It's been a pleasure to work with you. I'm glad to see you, my friend. Both of us, Henry. We could do it again at some point.

Relieved he was finally gone, I answered, "Sure."

Cathy shook his hand as she pushed a folded $20 into his. When she thanked him, he bowed, kissed her cheek, and departed.

"I despise jails because of what they do to people," Cathy stated as she shut the door behind her. A hand rested on her brow as she bowed. He used to be a clever man, albeit a little flaky, but he was still a sweetheart. What a waste he's become now. "

When Mom and I entered the living room, her face was distorted with grief. I knelt down next to her and held her hand as she screamed out her feelings of resentment. It's happened to me numerous times. To put it another way, a man with good intentions goes into that system and comes out of it utterly destroyed. Now, all I care about is keeping people out of jail. That's what I do for a living.

Even if they are guilty, it makes no difference to me. So that they don't become any worse, I just want to keep them out of those awful places. "

Do you remember him entering your bedroom last night? I resented asking, but I couldn't stop myself.

Incredulous, she fixed her gaze on me. She couldn't believe what was going through my mind. "No! And even if he did, I'd be able to cope. "

My brow furrowed and my eyes became narrowed. Do you mean to say that I should "manage it?" Is that what you wanted him to do? "

"What's up with you, Henry?" It's time to get off of it. " Her annoyed face shifted to one of concern as she peered into my face. "What happened to Dennis breaks my heart, and I feel horrible for him." But he's not mine. I'm not interested in him. I'd have thrown him out of my room if he'd tried to sneak into mine. The way I would have handled it is exactly how I would have done it. "

"Oh... OK." It made me feel better, and a little silly for getting so worked up in the first place. I assured myself that my father was not a threat.

However, a few days later, he contacted and persuaded her to go out to dinner with him and his mother "to reminisce about the past." While they went to our favorite Mexican restaurant, I stayed home and ate enchiladas from a can. A different location was an option. I was fuming, picturing them kissing over sangria, returning to her apartment, and doing all manner of heinous crimes. I felt unwelcome and unqualified—how could I ever compete with someone as charismatic as him? At the time, I was just a little boy. But I couldn't bring myself out of it, even though I knew I was having an unreasonable fit. Because we were in a two-person relationship, all of our interests were amplified. Jealousy and a sense of ownership were also squared.

For some reason, the concept of going along with an attractive woman to retaliate against her felt absurd. As a result of getting the actual thing, I'd been spoiled for girls.

When Cathy returned, I was watching Laugh-In with a grimace on my face. I made a conscious effort not to look her in the eyes. She took my hand and sat on the edge of the couch.

I'm curious to know what happened. I was able to utter my thoughts before they were stifled.

"There was no activity. We just had a conversation. "

Inquiringly, "Did you return to his residence?"

"Of course not!" I reply. She gave a shaky sigh. Isn't it true that you're really in hot water over this?

I was unable to speak because my jaw was clinched so tightly.

This is a Scorpio in every sense of the word: "God, you're so Scorpio." She shook me by the shoulders and gave me an embracing glance that melted the terror from my face. "Let's sit here for a minute and be quiet," she said.

Breathing was audible in the midst of the quiet. When she placed her hand on my shoulder, a calming stream flowed into my body. The two of us sat there for a while, relishing each other's company. This warm, throbbing closeness made the ecstasy more visceral, and our breathing got faster as we continued to keep in time with each other. When she rose up and squeezed my hand, I just followed her into her room without saying anything.

My mother grasped both of my hands in hers and squeezed them tightly. She said, "Take a look at me."

She had straight auburn hair, and her oval face was peaceful and full of affection, despite her stern expression. Her soft complexion radiated a luminosity that appeared to come from deep within her. Her bright brown eyes had crinkled corners. Her wide lips were furrowed by tiny wrinkles. Put your hand on your mother's chin and kiss her.

He felt the smooth warmth of her cheek when he placed his fingers there.

"Smooch my lips."

Her face appeared to enlarge to fill my vision as I got closer, and my lips rubbed against hers as we kissed. I felt a burst of light and chimes fill the hole that had been there for so long.

"Only you have my lips." They are not kissed by anybody else. " I caught a whiff of sangria and salsa as she spoke. I gave her another kiss.

She took a few steps backward to give herself some breathing room. What's going on here, Henry? You've got to see this. " The bulges in her batik blouse drew my gaze upwards as she pushed her chest outward. "It's time to unbutton."

I shivered my fingers as I unfastened her dress's wooden buttons. These women's cleavages were fuller and more prominent than ever before. Their lacy white bras were overflowing, they had dimples in their bellies, and their ribs were well below these beautifully cantilevered mounds.

"It's time to take my blouse off."

As soon as her arms were freed, I grabbed her tit with both hands and threw the rest away.

Cathy put her arms around them and sighed. "I'll tell you when I'm ready."

I bowed my head respectfully and lowered my hands.

Kiss me right here. She felt a small hollow at the base of her neck.

In my mind's eye, her thyroid was humming, keeping her in tune.

I've never had anyone else kiss me in that spot. You are the only one who can. It's yours to keep. "Kiss me now, please." She felt her breasts up to the point where they met her bra straps.

"Your time here has finally come." You are the only one

that kisses me there. " She placed her hands in a fist-like position under her bra. "Remove this now. It irritates me.

The clasp was easy to unhook now that I'd practiced a few times. I saw her tits take possession of her topside and her nipples were already stiff as the bra came off. They seemed to say, "Hello there." Please hug us.

My head sank as I made a move for them, but mom quickly snatched them away with her hands. "Until then, To begin, you'll need some information. With her fingers, she pushed my chin up until our eyes met. "There is no one else here but you. No one else has the privilege of sucking them up. " With her hands, she raised them up and presented them to me as a kind gift. "Here. They're yours. "

In my hands, I held each one, admiring its weight and opulence. One of them started chanting, "Me me me!" as

I kissed the other. Taking a sip and a smile, I moved between the two heavenly realms, where there was no worry. You need to get rid of your mother's trousers.

I sank to my knees in front of her, remorseful that we were parting yet eager for what she had left to offer.

However, before you do it, make sure to kiss her belly.

I could hear food gurgling under her padding as I pressed my cheek and ear against her tummy for a tighter hug. I licked and teased her belly button with my tongue as I kissed her in a circle around the soft cushion of her sHenryach.

"Tickles," she whispered, shivering in her seat.

When I was done licking her, I looked into her twisted omphalos and felt the enormous chain of navels extending from the first mother's womb back to Eve. No one would be alive if the first family hadn't been incestuous, so they must have been.

You're welcome to play with my tummy. Now let me get my pants off. "

To display a slice of the white abdomen, I unbuttoned and zipped up the jeans. I used to think I was inside there, all snuggled up to her. I began to pant as I kissed her pink underpants and smelled her fishy scent. When I peeled down the blue denim, I saw the black shadow of her pubic region peeking out from under the lace of her panties. I placed my lips reverently on the mound, allowing myself to inhale its scent and feel its warmth. Cathy removed her sandals from her feet. With my teeth nipping at her thighs, I nuzzled my head into her crotch as I lowered the pants further. Thank you, bones and cartilage, for all your hard work. I sucked her skin at her knees. While she was undressed, I licked her calves and ankles, and she walked out of the house in her underwear. I noticed an oval of wetness on her pink underwear as I retraced my steps.

There's only one person these legs want to wrap around: you. She stroked my head and smiled. Make me nude, then have the audacity to strip.

I placed her wet underpants back into her bra and massaged, lifted, squeezed, and kissed her full buns. My dick was so erect that it hurt because of the aroma of her musk. Her black kinky curls, big cheeks, and wet protruding lips that chirped a command: Adore me! were exposed as I ripped the silk from her center.

My underpants were gone after a long swipe. Her cousin's wet fuchsia ruffles drew my lips to hers, and I gasped as I licked them. The answer is definitely yes! Her sexy scent beckoned to my senses as I sifted through her hair. My fingers slid into her groin from behind, widening the entrance.

"My pussy is only for you," my mother promised me from the heavens. "None of these things are allowed to be done by anyone other than you." It's now yours. " She stroked my hair with her fingers.

I kissed her thighs goodbye and rose to my feet. As our eyes met, they formed a channel of trust. My heart ached within my jeans as I glanced down at her gorgeous bare body. I was so impressed by her generosity that I felt compelled to reciprocate. I urged her to remove her son's clothes. "Distract him."

She ripped off my T-shirt, rubbing her fingers across my chest while I raised my arms. So she said, "OK, if I cop a feel."

As I nodded, her hands squeezed firmly on top of my shoulders, chest, and biceps. "You're a fighter!" she exclaimed.

"You gave me the strength to face the world."

When she said it, she meant, "I want to make you right now!" Both Cathy and I liked how soft she was compared to how hard I was, so I gently squeezed her tit between my upper and lower arm muscles while she bit me on the neck.

"Then I'm yours." I'm only here for you. " To her, I made a solemn oath.

They were at my waist, pulling at the metal buttons on my jeans as she caressed my sHenryach. While my white-steepled underpants announced, "I'm next," heavy denim tumbled to my ankles as they came undone. It's my turn now!

When she started stroking her finger on the tip of the tented cotton, it became wetter. I shivered with delight as she gave it small pinches on the head and the shaft. When I was a kid, my mom used to ask me, "What's in there?"

Before I could begin speaking, I had to take a sip of water. "You'll have to find out for yourself."

Pulling back the elastic, her eyes went wide with fear. It looks like you've got a strange, large object inside! To what end? "

"It's up to you to discover."

"Doubtful if I want to do it at all. You never know. "

Not at all. "

"Promise?"

"Promise."

"Good. That's right! " As soon as she pulled her pants down, the creature swung out, its one moist eye fixated on her. One of her hands went to her chest as she uttered, "Oh." "What's the point of this?"

I said, "You," and she looked at me in surprise. It's solely interested in you. You're the only one who can use it. "

Almost as if she were handling a gigantic and potentially deadly animal, she gingerly extended her fingers to make contact. Why is it trying to harm me?

I comforted her by gently stroking her shoulders. "Take a look inside of yourself. You are the only one who can see it. "

"Well... OK. If and only if you so specify. What happens to it? "

I caressed her swollen, puddle-drenched heart. I'm just over here. It's right where it should be. "

Her expression was tense. Instead of waiting until I feel too scared, give it to me now.

It's time for you to get some shut-eye.

Cathy sank to her knees, her juicy red cunt exposed, her legs spread out in front of her. "How about this?"

As if by magic. Before I could put on any clothes, I had to take them off first.

She asked, her voice soft and innocent.

I knelt down between her ankles on the bed. "Perhaps a little."

"Oh!" When she closed her knees and bit her large botHenry lip with her small white teeth, she looked like she was about to cry.

Her knees were exposed. "First and foremost,"

When it happens, what happens next?

That's when you'll like it. "

"OK. Put in a little at a time, though. "Slowly but surely," she said with a sulk.

I crept up on her in between her thighs. In her panic, she gnawed on the quilt as my prong approached, eyes shut tight and face scrunched.

Using my index finger, I placed it between her lips. Do you feel any pain as a result of that? I inquired, my body trembling in ecstasy at the touch.

"It won't work if you take your time."

When it came to slithering inside her sexy vagina, the process had to be slow and long-winded, and I loved every millimeter of it.

Mom murmured under her breath, "I'm full," her lips puffing up.

"Good. exactly as you're meant to be. When it's my job to fill you up, I'll do it. "

"Oh." She wiggled around it. "It appeals to me."

I brought it out again.

She yelled, "Don't go away!"

When you say, "I'll be back," you mean it.

"OK."

Ahead of her portal arch, I gently massaged the head

around its circumference, pressing it into the delicate frills and nodes. Then I sank very slowly back into ecstasy, opening her up again.

You're torturing me, aren't you? Her screams faded into a groan.

I assured her, "I'm only going to do it for you." For me, there's only one woman like you.

I felt my mother's legs wrap around my back as she held me close in her arms. I wrapped my arms around her and snuggled her close to me. Her titters fell toward her shoulders as she leaned this way, and I sucked one into my lips.

Slow thrusts swayed her back and forth as I entered and exited. Insatiable, her hands pounced on my head, my back, and the back of my thigh. The love that comes from a vow of loyalty can be seen in our gazes as we looked into each other's eyes. I managed to mutter, "Thank you... for being mine."

"My goodness! You've snatched me off the street. This is your lady. "

"Yeah... and I'm the one for the job." I pumped her harder, slamming into her, desperate to have her all to myself, as if punishing her in some way for having ever made out with anybody other than me. Taking a deep breath, she arched her back against mine and leaned towards me, savoring the sensation.

"That's a real pain in the a**." It's making me want to come, oh! "She screamed in astonishment. At the same time as her inner muscles tensely gripped me, her pelvis arose to meet each of my hammering thrusts. When our hairy middles fused together, we formed a creature that was larger than either of us. A series of long striations appeared on my back as her nails sank into my skin.

My elation was heightened by the sting. Driving faster and harder, I slammed into her, sending her flying through the air and out of control. We came together in a swirling mass of screaming bodies, grappling and wrestling, and becoming one.

After a long battle, we collapsed exhausted on the ground. You're such a great scumbag, you know it. You've hit the nail on the head with this one, haven't you? "Finally, mom remarked, "After that, I'll no longer be able to call you Henry." Henry now a certainty. Henry is a male beast, hence he's my guy! "

She put her head on my shoulder and kissed me goodnight. Whenever I'm with you, you make me feel like a little girl, like I'm just beginning to understand how the world works down there... It's become a lot more dynamic. " Cathy squinted her eyes at her and shook her head. After that, I'll go to my place. In comparison to hers, mine had shrunk greatly. In between her beautiful lips, what I had put in hers was now dripping out. Both of us appeared content and in control as we slumbered.

To make me feel more secure, Mom put her breasts in my face. "Do it all over again. It's a huge hit with them. " She continued to speak, but now frightened, as I eagerly took them into my mouth. "In the past, haven't you had any fun with other women? And you've done it all with girls, right? Are you a woman? What about me? "

After a few more kisses, I decided to lay my cheek on her tit instead. "You're the only one who matters here."

How far did you go with the other girls? She sounded as

if she didn't want to ask but was obliged to do so because she couldn't help it. "How about those breasts?"

"Sometimes."

"What's going on down there?"

"Once." I was embarrassed and angry that she was getting in the way of my personal life in this way.

"Who were they with?" I inquired.

"What's the point?"

She cradled me as if I were about to vanish. It may be that I'm envious. I'm not sure if I'm just torturing myself. Who or what is stalking my boy? "

I climbed out of her chest and sat on my elbow. It's possible I was pursuing her. Mom's flinch made her look older because it highlighted the wrinkles around her eyes and mouth. However, "I'm not after her anymore," I said, assuring her. That's all because I wasn't with you. I'm sorry.

She gave me a big hug and appeared relieved. "I apologize for the inconvenience. The fact that you specify that you just want me there means a lot to me. The others can go to hell. "

As I said, "Alright." "Just the two of us."

Cathy burst into a little weary chuckle. "Isn't it difficult?"

But it's worth it, she says.

As we rested in each other's arms, I reflected on the weight of the vow we had made. We are now a married couple, and we couldn't be happier. It was a touch frightening, but it had a richer, more substantial feel to it. We had reached a new level of dedication as a result of

Dennis's threat.

# Acknowledgments

The Glory of this book's success goes to God Almighty and my beautiful Family, Fans, Readers & well-wishers, CusHenryers, and Friends for their endless support and encouragement

# About The Author

My name is Luca Lincoln, and I'm an erotica writer and reader. There's nothing better for me than knowing that you've enjoyed my stories, which explore the extremes of sexual pleasure. Enjoy the sexiness and strength of the darkness. My favorite part is the intensity and ferocity. I admire a man's determination to achieve his goals, no matter the cost. As a result of my fascination with both the current world and the characters that inhabit it, I write both fantasy and contemporary romance as well. I'm a big fan of the modern family and modern partnerships. Writing romantic stories is something I've always wanted to do. My goal as a writer is to bring my passion for romantic fiction to a wider audience.

Lightning Source UK Ltd.
Milton Keynes UK
UKHW022314070223
416656UK00023B/341